RIKK
OF THE
RENDAL
CLAN

Books by Borghild Dahl

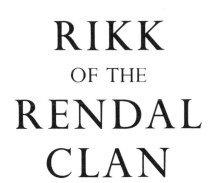

RIKK
OF THE
RENDAL
CLAN

by
Borghild Dahl

Illustrated by
Ib Ohlsson

E. P. DUTTON & CO., INC. NEW YORK

First Edition

*For my grandnieces, Ingrid and Elizabeth Eliasson,
and for my grandnephews, Scott, Stewart and Thomas
Ramsey, and Mark Shafer*

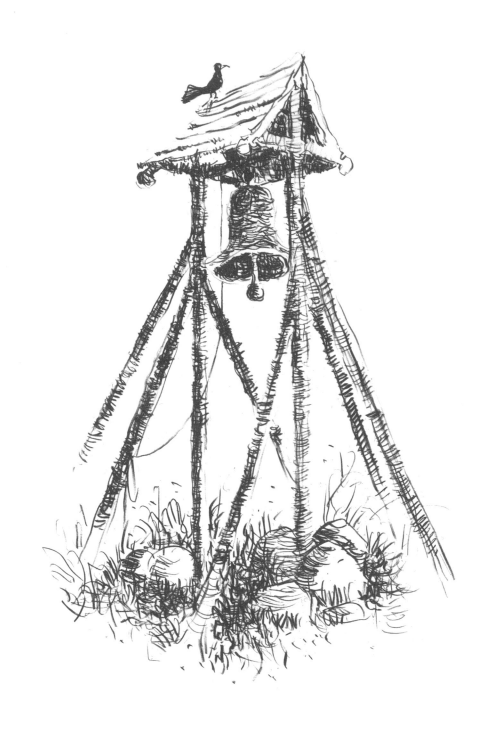

Rikk rubbed his eyes. It was morning.

He sat up and his heart began to beat faster. For this was a very special morning. In fact, it was the most important day of his whole life.

Today, Rikk was twelve years old. He had come of age, and this, as every troll knew well, meant that he was to undergo a test. He was to set out all by himself on a journey that, if successful, would give him the right to be classed among the grownups of his clan.

Today Rikk would be sent out of the cave in which he lived with all the other members of the Rendal clan in the great Oster Valley. He would go alone. And if the report he brought back was satisfactory . . . Rikk trembled with excitement at what lay ahead of him.

When Spinster Great-aunt Aasve had announced that it was
time for Rikk to make his first trip into the outside world, she
had said that he must have an outfit suitable for the occasion.
He must no longer wear the one-piece sacklike gray garment
that covered the children of the clan from top to toe.

As soon as Rikk's mother heard this pronouncement, she
had gone outside to look for the soft wisps of lamb's wool that
were purposely left for the trolls in the sheepshed of the
Ringsgaard estate. She washed and carded the wool, spinning
and dyeing the yarn, and her loom hummed from morning to
night weaving beautiful lengths of fine wool cloth.

Rikk dressed himself slowly and with great care, and at last he stood resplendent. His red coat was embroidered with the letter R, the insignia of the Rendal clan, on the right side of his chest. He had bright green trousers, golden-brown leggings, and, for a crowning touch, a peaked cap of bright red. This was not only wonderful in itself but it added to his height, which was six inches. It occurred to Rikk that if he should meet an animal or a human being while he was on the road, he could also make himself look taller by walking on tiptoe.

He wished that his eyes had been brown instead of blue, and that his hair was darker to set off his cap. Nevertheless, if he had been wearing a king's robe and a golden crown he could not have been more pleased with his general appearance.

Rikk was too excited to eat much of the breakfast of fine chopped pine cones and dewdrops, which was his favorite breakfast and which his mother had prepared especially for the occasion. When the meal was finally over and the family

brushed aside the cobweb partition that separated their room from the others in the cave, his knees shook under him.

In the great hall at the mouth of the cave, a goodly number of the clan had already assembled. For no troll of the Rendal clan was ever allowed to venture forth into adult life without the good wishes of every man, woman and child who belonged to it.

"It scarcely seems possible, Reider," said Grandmother Rendal, coming over to Rikk's father, "that your baby has come of age. It seems only yesterday that I dandled you, my son, on my knee, and now our youngest . . ."

Rikk did not hear the rest of the sentence, for at that moment there was a great commotion from farther inside the cave. There was a murmur of hushed voices, and Rikk knew that this greeting of subdued awe was never accorded to anyone but Spinster Great-aunt Aasve.

She came in leaning on a cane, but otherwise, in spite of her age, she gave an impression of tremendous vigor and alertness. Today there was a smile on her lips and she singled out Rikk immediately. She directed her steps toward him, putting her willow-stem cane down on the stone floor of the cave with a determined thump.

"So this is your day, Rikk," she said. "Now let us see if you remember the lessons I have been teaching you all these years."

"I have been thinking," Rikk's mother said a trifle tremulously, "that it might be better if we postponed his journey for another year. You know he is the youngest, and not so robust, and—"

"Now, Blomster," Spinster Great-aunt Aasve interrupted her severely, "don't you go putting any foolish notions into Rikk's head. Even though he is slightly smaller than your other twelve children, his mind is as keen as any of theirs. And that is what will count in the outside world."

Rikk saw a tear in his mother's eye and turned away, pretending not to notice. Nothing must stop him from setting out on his adventure.

As was her custom, Spinster Great-aunt Aasve began to conduct the final examination. "What is the most important thing you must remember?" she asked.

"That no sunbeam must ever shine on me," Rikk said.

"And if it does?" she queried.

"Don't frighten the child by making him answer," Rikk's older sister begged.

"You know the answer, don't you?" Spinster Great-aunt Aasve insisted.

"Yes," said Rikk boldly. "No more a troll."

As far back as he could remember, he had heard about the fate of his sixteenth cousin, to whom just such a calamity had occurred. The moment the sun had struck him he had disappeared into thin air and had never been heard of since, and

it was known by the trolls of all Norway that they must never let the full sun shine upon them.

"Well said, Rikk," said Spinster Great-aunt Aasve approvingly. "And what else is of importance?"

"If I tap behind my left ear," said Rikk, "I will be able to talk to any animal, bird or fish in his own language."

"Don't forget that this also applies to bugs and other small creatures," Spinster Great-aunt Aasve reminded him.

"It is also important that I be able to understand what human beings say," said Rikk proudly, "although I must never be seen by them. To understand their speech, I must tap behind my *right* ear."

13

"Good," said Spinster Great-aunt Aasve. "But I must caution you about human beings. Some of them are very peculiar about their speech. Here in Oster Valley, people speak intelligently, but in my travels I have come across strangers—" She shrugged. "There is no sense in what comes out of their mouths, twisting their tongues as they do. But don't worry about that. It is autumn now, and no outsiders are apt to venture our way."

Rikk was anxious to put an end to the examination, but Spinster Great-aunt Aasve took her time. "How far are you to go today?" she asked.

"Until I reach the crossroads," Rikk answered promptly.

"And why there?" she demanded.

"Because all the roads from then on lead to where—well, I'm not supposed to—"

"You are right. If you continued straight on, you would be headed for the high mountains to the north. To the left, you would find yourself in no time on a high cliff beyond which would be the turbulent Glommen River. And to the west, the sea, great cities—no, remember at all costs to turn back at the crossroads."

"Perhaps he had better turn back as soon as he reaches the Ringsgaard estate," his mother said timidly.

"Now, Blomster," Spinster Great-aunt Aasve exclaimed severely, "I have estimated the time with great care. It is early morning now. If Rikk keeps walking steadily, he will reach the crossroads and be back to the Ringsgaard estate just as they sound the great bell to bring the men in from the fields for their noon dinner. The bell will be a little late now, since the days are short and the men will not go out again in the afternoon for the fall ploughing."

"And what has the bell to do with me?" asked Rikk, who had been listening attentively.

"This. When the bell rings, you should be well on your homeward way. You should be passing the estate on your return trip when it begins to peal. There is no mistaking it. It can be heard for miles."

"I'll try my best," Rikk said.

"I shall expect your best."

"I am sure I can do it," said Rikk confidently. Now that Spinster Great-aunt Aasve had put a time limit to this journey as a test of his ability to behave in a grown-up manner, he was more anxious than ever to be off.

"One more thing before you go," she said, and she drew from her voluminous pocket something soft and gray. She shook it out and it turned out to be a large cloak of some sort. "I gathered thistledown in distant parts, spun it and wove it.

It is so thin as to be almost invisible, as you can see. But it is as strong as iron, or the heaviest of skins. No sunbeam will ever penetrate it, no rain can soak it, and if you cover yourself with it, no one will be able to single you out from the landscape. Put it in your pocket and guard it as carefully as your life."

"Thank you. And now may I leave?" Rikk asked eagerly.

Rikk's father and his Uncle Tork pushed away the heavy door that had completely filled up the opening of the cave. The sound of the waterfall outside nearly drowned the voices of all his relatives, wishing him good luck, and with one leap he found himself outside, ready to start on his journey.

Behind him, the great stone door swung shut, and for the first time in his life, Rikk was alone.

R ikk drew a deep breath.

Big Brother Skog, who had charge of the weather report for the Rendal clan, had said that the sky was heavily overcast and that fog lay over the valley. But even so, the light of the outside world in contrast to the dimness of the cave was astounding. In fact, Rikk had to open and close his eyes several times before he could take in what lay about him.

The beautiful greenness of the grass was perhaps the most astonishing. Spinster Great-aunt Aasve had described the colors of the outside world in great detail to him, but he could never have imagined such splendor as the grass displayed.

And then there was the waterfall. Always, day and night, he had heard its roar from inside the cave, but to see it and hear it so close at hand was breathtaking. For a moment, as

19

he looked at it, it seemed to Rikk that the outside world consisted of nothing but water, roaring, tumbling water with its foam and noise. No wonder there were all sorts of tales about who or what caused its never-ending power.

He backed away a little, still looking at the waterfall and the miracle of the foaming water. Even if he saw nothing but this, he would have had an experience worth telling about after he was home again.

It must have been his awe at the waterfall that caused Rikk to lose for a moment his sense of direction, but the next thing he knew was that he found himself in the midst of green weeds. They loomed so high above his head that he could not see where he was. The situation was most disconcerting, and for a moment he felt almost a sense of fear.

Then, down on the ground just ahead of him he heard a slight noise. A kind of chirping sound. Only crickets, Spinster Great-aunt Aasve had told him, used this kind of language.

Rikk made a quick movement of his left hand and tapped the back of his left ear. At once he was able to understand what the cricket was trying to say, and the knowledge that he was already putting his instructions to use restored his self-confidence. It was really miraculous, he told himself proudly.

"Please be careful," the cricket was saying. "I am just ahead of you. Please be careful not to step on me."

Rikk felt even more confident. Crickets were messengers of good luck and it was an omen of good fortune that a cricket was the first living creature he had met on his journey.

"If you had stepped on me," the cricket went on, "it would most likely have been the end of me."

Rikk was at once filled with remorse. "I am so sorry," he exclaimed. "Believe me, I am. It was only that the daylight dazzled me, and I must have lost my way."

"You don't need to apologize," said the cricket in a more friendly tone. "It is just that we crickets are in constant danger of being stepped on, especially by human beings. Most of them have absolutely no feeling for us small creatures."

"Oh, but we trolls do," Rikk said. "That is why I am being sent out into the world today. I am to learn to conduct myself properly, like all the members of the Rendal clan, so that I will be grown up and can be of help to all living creatures."

"That is certainly a worthy philosophy of life," the cricket said admiringly. "I do believe that I have met with several of your elders, and always they have shown the greatest consideration. Usually, however, they keep to a trodden path or

the main road, both of which we crickets have been taught
from infancy to avoid."

"Since you feel so kindly toward my family," said Rikk,
"perhaps you will show me the way to the main road."

"With pleasure," the cricket agreed. "Only remain at a safe
enough distance so that if I stop suddenly you won't step on
me."

Rikk thanked the cricket, and the two started off. The
cricket was a most cheerful creature, and as they went along
he chirped merrily.

"I shall certainly tell my Spinster Great-aunt Aasve about
your kindness," Rikk said gratefully.

"Oh, you needn't bother. As I told you, we crickets and you
trolls are great friends. We are always glad to do favors for
each other when an opportunity presents itself."

Soon the tall green blades of the weeds were farther and farther apart, and the light of day became brighter once more. Rikk hoped that the sun was not going to come out.

Just to make sure he asked the cricket, "You don't see any sunbeams, do you?"

The cricket chuckled. "Oh, no, this is one of the darkest days we have had so far this fall."

That, at least, was a consolation. Rikk had begun to realize why his mother was so fearful about his starting out. Still, he could not stay home and be classed as the runt who didn't know enough to grow up.

Suddenly an expanse of gray appeared ahead of them.

"Well, here we are on the main road," the cricket said. "Do you happen to remember in what direction you are supposed to be traveling?"

"Oh, yes," Rikk assured him. "I am to follow the road until I come to the crossroads. Beyond that it would lead up into the mountains where the peaks are already capped with snow. In other directions I would reach the River Glommen or the great cities and the sea."

"Gracious," said the cricket. "So much geography in a single head. Fortunately, there is no need for my learning all such facts. All I have to do is to keep in the tall grass and stay away from feet, large or small. I'm glad there is nothing more I need to know."

For a moment, Rikk almost envied the cricket his simple life. But then he remembered the many exciting exploits he had heard about from his elders, and the thrill of adventure returned to him.

24

True enough, the expanse of the road stretching out ahead of him seemed overpowering, but the greater the challenge the greater would be the satisfaction of returning to the cave with his journey accomplished.

Rikk took one long breath and counted to thirteen. This was his lucky number, since he was the thirteenth child of his parents. Then he said good-bye to the cricket and started out alone, to walk in the middle of the great expanse of road.

For a while Rikk trudged on steadily.

It was a beautiful place, this outside world where people and birds and animals lived. On both sides of the road, white-stemmed birches tossed their silvery-green leaves against the more somber green of the pines and hemlocks, and the ground was bright with purple heather. His Spinster Great-aunt Aasve knew the names of all the trees and flowers that grew outside the cave, and she had been a thorough teacher to all the younger people of their clan for three or four generations. Rikk was proud now that he was able to recognize everything he saw as he walked along.

Ahead of him there was something moving, and Rikk knew at once what it was. It was a frog. A real live one. Rikk had heard all about frogs, but he had had no idea how wonderful it was to jump as this frog was doing. In two leaps, the frog was at his side.

26

Rikk tapped his left ear so quickly that he almost knocked off his cap. At once the croaking of the frog made sense.

"Good morning," the frog said, "although I wouldn't say it is a very good morning. For the sky is heavy and the air is full of fog and mist."

"In that I must differ with you," said Rikk. "For it is exactly the sort of weather that makes life bearable—" He stopped himself. After all, Rikk thought, growing suddenly cautious, it was not necessary to give away all the life secrets of trolls. That was a warning which Spinster Great-aunt Aasve had repeated more than once.

"Everyone to his taste," said the frog. "I must say we frogs do not look forward to winter. Cold weather does not agree with us."

While he spoke he kept jumping hither and yon, away from Rikk and then back to his side.

"I must say you do jump most gracefully," Rikk said admiringly.

"It's a most convenient way of getting places at great speed," said the frog, hopping off again.

"If I could hop, I would be able to reach the crossroads in far less time than by walking," Rikk said regretfully.

The frog returned to Rikk's side. "Let's try it out. You walk and I'll jump, and we'll see who can go the fastest."

The two started out. Rikk made every effort to keep up, but the frog went so fast he was almost out of sight. Then he jumped back to Rikk's side.

"You see how foolish you are to keep to your way of moving," the frog said. "Now just learn the art of jumping and you will find that it makes all the difference."

Rikk put all the strength he could into the attempt and jumped. He jumped and jumped. But, to his disappointment, he found that he made even less progress, if anything, than when he was walking. And the effort of jumping was so great that soon he was out of breath.

"I guess I had better go back to my walking," he managed to say to the frog.

"There is no use trying to teach a troll anything," said the frog, and away he went, hopping along at a great speed.

Rikk was too tired even to walk for a moment and he sat down beside the road to rest. It was certainly a great disappointment to find that even a frog could beat him.

After a while, however, Rikk felt more optimistic. If Spinster Great-aunt Aasve had felt that jumping was the right way to move, she would certainly have given him lessons. After all, each creature had its own way of getting around in the world, and even if his way took a longer time he would get to the crossroads eventually.

Rikk got up and set out once more. Spinster Great-aunt Aasve had taught him to count, and to help himself forget the slow passage of time, he began to speak aloud. "One, two, three, four, five, six." But the mere effort of raising his voice was an extra exertion, and he also began to realize that he was getting hungry. If only he had had a second helping of the delicious breakfast that his mother had so thoughtfully prepared for him. For a moment he almost wished himself back in the safety of the cave, where everything had been done for him.

It would help a great deal, Rikk decided, if he knew how far it still was to the crossroads.

From the side of the road a bird had been watching him. It was a sparrow, and it flew away as Rikk drew nearer.

Quickly, Rikk tapped his left ear and called loudly, "Don't fly away, Mr. Sparrow. Please don't."

The sparrow stopped and approached Rikk slowly. Rikk slackened his own gait to assure the bird of his good intentions.

"I am on my way to the crossroads," Rikk told the sparrow after they had exchanged greetings. "Can you tell me how far away it is?"

"That I cannot," said the sparrow regretfully, "since I usually keep to the woods. But if you were to climb to the top of the pine tree yonder, you would be able to find out."

"But I don't know how to climb a tree," Rikk objected. "We learned how to climb rocks inside the cave where we Rendal trolls make our home, but that was different. They were broad and the ascent was easy. There were no trees in our cave, you understand."

"Climbing a tree is very simple," the sparrow said. "Just watch me for an instant. I will teach you in no time how to do it."

The sparrow flew into the woods to a tree and hopped from branch to branch until he had almost reached the top. "See," he called out, "if I were to climb a little farther, I would be able to look out over the entire landscape."

31

"But I have no wings," Rikk objected.

"They won't be necessary," said the sparrow. "Just climb from branch to branch."

Rikk hesitated. If he tried to climb the tree it would mean a delay in reaching his goal. On the other hand, it would be a great help to know how much farther he had to travel.

"You don't mean to say that you trolls lack the courage of mere cats?" the sparrow asked.

"It isn't that. But I have never had any practice in tree climbing."

"There is always a first time for everything," the sparrow said.

It was almost as though the sparrow was daring him to try, and Rikk had never been one to refuse a dare. In fact, his mother had cautioned him more than once to be more careful, and this was one of the reasons she had begged Spinster Great-aunt Aasve to have him wait another year. To give him the stable judgment of an older person, she had explained.

"It is easy," the sparrow said again.

Rikk felt that he had to know how much farther he had to go, and so he approached the tree. The trunk was rough and full of sharp points, and the pine needles scratched his face and hands. Yet he kept on climbing, hoping that things would soon get easier, and for every branch he reached, the sparrow hopped easily to the one above.

Then he looked down, which was a great mistake. He became dizzy, and before he could collect his wits he felt himself falling. The heavy branches slowed him down as he tried

to catch at them, and the pine needles on the forest floor broke his fall when he landed in them, but all the same he nearly had the breath knocked out of him.

When he was finally able to get up, he looked around. The sparrow had disappeared.

Rikk realized how foolish he had been, taking advice that was absolutely wrong for him. Spinster Great-aunt Aasve had told him to walk in the middle of the road until he reached the crossroads, and if he had taken her advice he would be nearly there by now.

He tried to forget how hungry and thirsty he was as he turned and began to trudge back to the road. The one important rule to remember from now on was not to stop for anything, no matter what it was.

L 1809014

It was easy to walk on the soft pine needles of the forest and Rikk had almost made his way back to the road when suddenly he stopped short. Ahead of him was a reddish glow, and for a moment he thought it must be the sun.

Rikk was about to turn and run as fast as he could into the depths of the forest. It would be a disaster for him to end his life almost before it had begun. Well, he'd take one quick look anyway. He would at least have the satisfaction of knowing what the sun looked like.

To his amazement it began to move toward him and he saw that it was not the sun after all, in spite of its color, for it had four feet and a tail.

Rikk was so frightened that he felt his teeth beginning to chatter, and well they might. He had been given careful lessons about all the animals of the forest, and he recognized at once the reddish-brown color, the long, sharp nose and the bushy tail. It was a fox.

35

The fox was the most immense living creature Rikk had ever seen, and he knew very well how dangerous it was. Spinster Great-aunt Aasve had warned him of its craftiness and its long, sharp teeth, and how greatly it was feared by all the other animals.

For a moment, Rikk was too frightened to try to make out what the fox was saying—it was only a strange noise. Then he recovered his wits enough to tap his left ear, and at once the noise became intelligible.

"Good morning," the fox was saying, and Rikk had to admit that the words were spoken in the politest manner possible.

It was necessary to respond in the same way. To show anger or fear would be fatal. That much he had been told over and over again by Spinster Great-aunt Aasve in her

lectures on troll behavior. So, trying his best to control his voice, Rikk replied, "Good morning, Mr. Fox. I am very happy to meet you this beautiful morning."

The fox smiled. "Not nearly as happy as I am to meet you. For today is a special day, it being the birthday of my dear wife, Madame Fox."

Rikk did his best to keep his voice steady. "Then we have something in common, Madame Fox and I, since it is my birthday too. I am celebrating my coming of age."

The fox smiled again. "Then we all have even more in common, for I am on my way to prepare for her birthday celebration."

Rikk took one cautious step backward, and the fox in his turn moved a little nearer.

"I am seeking," said the fox, "a toothsome morsel for her birthday dinner. She has long been a faithful and devoted wife to me, and there is nothing she would enjoy more than one of the famous Rendal trolls on her table."

Rikk felt his heart beating so loudly that he was sure the fox must be hearing it. Well, let it beat. He wasn't going to let himself be turned into a dinner if he could help it.

But at the moment, all he could think of to do was to keep the conversation going. "At what time do you propose to serve this delicious meal to her?" he asked, his throat so dry that he could hardly speak.

"My wife," said the fox, "prefers to dine at noon."

He moved forward another step, and at that moment Rikk remembered the gray cloak that Spinster Great-aunt Aasve had given him. But it was folded in his pocket, and if he tried to pull it out, the fox would spring on him. He steadied his thoughts. What he needed was a trick to pull the fox's attention away for a moment.

"You are most fortunate to live in this part of the forest," Rikk said, trying hard to keep his voice from quivering. "It is famous for all the wildlife that abounds in it."

"I am not interested in wildlife," said the fox curtly.

"Perhaps not," said Rikk, "but there are those who are. You have not heard, perhaps, of the wolves that have been coming down from Finland."

"Wolves?" said the fox, staring at him.

"There is a lack of food in Finland," said Rikk, "and the wolves are starving. They heard there was food in Norway, and packs of the hungry beasts have been making their way south into the Oster Valley."

There was no doubt that the fox was paying attention now. "Where did you get this story?" he said.

"I heard it yesterday in our cave. My uncle heard it from—" He jerked back suddenly and shrieked, "Look out! The wolf! He's right behind you."

The fox whirled around and at that moment Rikk pulled the gray cloak out of his pocket, shook it out and dropped down underneath it. Then he lay there under his covering, scarcely daring to breathe and not moving a muscle.

Rikk could hear the fox walking in circles around him. "That troll was standing right here," he said to himself. "I know he was."

Around and around he kept walking. "And that stone. I know it wasn't there before. My wits must be failing me."

Rikk lay without moving. There was a whining in the fox's voice now.

"I can't return to my wife with nothing but a stone to offer her for the birthday feast. It would be the end of our marriage."

At last there were no further mutterings, and it seemed to Rikk that the fox must have gone away. Still, Rikk knew that he could not take any chances. The fox might be waiting for him silently, and he would have to stay quiet under the cloak until he was absolutely sure it was safe to venture out.

It might have been hours, or even all night for all Rikk knew, before he decided that he could not stay under his covering forever. He would have to take a chance and make a dash for the safety of the open road, where the fox would not follow him.

He poked his head out, and there was no sign of the fox. On the alert every second, Rikk moved cautiously, the magic covering clutched firmly in his right hand in case there was any sign of danger.

Once he thought he heard footsteps behind him, but it was only the wind in the pine boughs.

Would he ever reach the road? Even the sound of his own breathing frightened him. Finally only a few steps remained before he would be out of the forest.

He broke into a run, and found himself at last on the open road.

For a moment Rikk stood still, and then he folded the covering carefully and put it back in his pocket. If it had not been for the gift that Spinster Great-aunt Aasve had given him, there would no longer be a troll named Rikk of the Rendal clan.

All he had to do now was to walk straight ahead, as fast as he could, until he came to the crossroads. He was still hungry and thirsty and tired, but he would forget about that now that he was so near to his goal.

Turning resolutely and looking straight ahead, Rikk started out once more, and as he put inch after inch of the road behind him, his good spirits returned.

After all, in spite of his misadventures, he had not done so badly. For one thing, he knew what a fox was like, and he couldn't help but admire its appearance. Moreover, he would never again let himself be caught in the depths of the forest, any more than he would ever try to jump like a frog or climb a tree like a bird.

By this time he had reached the end of the thick dark forest that had bordered the road to the right, and he knew from Spinster Great-aunt Aasve's instructions that he was near the Ringsgaard estate. He would have liked to stop, for the trolls of the Rendal clan were the friends of all the farm animals there, but he knew that he must not, and in fact he quickened his pace.

Rikk did, however, cast a furtive glance to his right to see what kind of houses were lived in by human beings. They certainly chose a peculiar type of living quarters—high, box-like things reaching up into the sky. He was glad that the Rendal clan could enjoy a real home in the safety of a cave.

Rikk would have liked to learn more, but he kept his gaze resolutely on the road ahead of him, and he had nearly reached a turn in the road when he heard the barking of a dog.

Instinctively Rikk put his hand to his left ear and then quickly drew it away. No, he must not try to find out what the dog was saying. That might involve him in another adventure, and at the moment this was the last thing he wanted.

The barking of the dog grew louder, and finally Rikk turned his head.

The dog was right behind him now, and so enormous that for a moment it seemed to Rikk that all the world was nothing but dog. Four gigantic legs held up such a huge body that Rikk had to tip his head back to see all of it.

Rikk knew at once what the dog was. It was a white Norwegian elkhound.

Now it happened that of all living creatures, Spinster Greataunt Aasve loved elkhounds the best, especially when they were snow white. She always spoke of them lovingly and could not praise too highly their admirable qualities. She usually finished by saying that not only did an elkhound possess all the virtues, but he was also the most beautiful and graceful of all the animals in the outside world. The elkhound, she said, always reminded her of a wedding guest, dressed to take part in the marriage festivities in an outfit of white fur from head to foot.

This elkhound, however, certainly did not look as though he were on his way to a wedding. His paws were black with mud, and he was wet as though he had been dipped in a pool of water.

The dog continued to bark, and when Rikk tried to continue walking the dog came in front of him and blocked his way. So, finally, Rikk tapped his left ear.

"Come quickly," the elkhound was saying.

"That I cannot do," said Rikk, not wanting to hear any more. "I am on my way to the crossroads, and because there have been many delays I am not nearly as far along as I should be."

The voice of the elkhound grew more insistent. "Come quickly," he said. "I must have your help."

"I will help you on my way home," said Rikk, "if I find that I am making good time."

"No," said the elkhound abruptly, "that will be too late. I will lie down on the ground so that you can climb up on my back. Hold on to my fur and there will be no danger of your falling off."

"No," said Rikk firmly.

The earnestness of the elkhound was beyond belief. "Please," he pleaded. "It will mean the death of my little master if you refuse."

There was no question of the truth of what he was saying, for such dogs never lied. With a sinking heart, Rikk scrambled up on the huge back. At once the elkhound got to his feet and started down a path through a thicket.

As he ran, he told Rikk what had happened. His master, little Petter Ringsgaard, had left the house and strayed down to the stream. The little boy knew the path because in winter he was allowed to sit on top of the load of logs that had been cut in the forest and were being taken down to the stream in a sleigh. When the stream gave up its winter ice, the logs were floated down to the great River Glommen and from there to the sawmills.

There were always a few logs left along the edge of the
stream and Petter had climbed on to one of them. Then it
had broken loose and floated out to midstream, where it was
caught by some reeds. The elkhound had missed his four-
year-old master and gone in search of him. He found him
clinging to the log, and in tears.

"He is so frightened," said the elkhound, "that I don't dare
to try and pull him off. I am afraid that when I try to get
him to shore by holding on to his clothes, he might turn face
downward accidentally and be drowned."

"What do you want me to do?" Rikk asked.

"You trolls understand the talk of human beings," the elk-hound said. "I want you to tell little Petter to slip on my back so that I can swim to shore with him."

"That is impossible," said Rikk firmly. "We trolls are not permitted to be seen by human beings." This was one of the strictest laws of the clan, and from his earliest years Rikk had known that it must never be broken.

By this time the elkhound had reached the edge of the stream, and Rikk could see little Petter.

In his mind's eye Rikk had pictured hundreds of times how

48

children must look, with their beautiful curly hair and their faces wreathed in smiles. Therefore it was quite a shock to see the small weeping boy clinging desperately to his log.

His face was stained with dirt and tears, his clothes were torn, and there were holes in his black knit stockings. Still, he was a real human being and the wonder of seeing one was something that any troll would remember forever.

"The log will not stay in those reeds very long," said the elkhound. "The current will carry it downstream, and my master with it."

"What do you want me to do?" Rikk asked desperately.

"I want you to tell him I am going to swim out. Tell him that he must stop crying and climb up on my back."

Rikk swallowed hard. There was no help for it. He could not remain silent and leave little Petter to drown.

He tapped his right ear.

"Petter," he called. "Can you hear me?"

For a moment the child stopped crying. Then he began again, louder than ever.

"Listen," said Rikk, "I am a troll. Do you know what a troll is?"

At once the wailing stopped. "Oh, yes," the little boy said. "My Uncle Lars told me that if I am a good boy the trolls will bring me a sled for Christmas."

"So they will," said Rikk. "I will see to it myself."

"We must hurry," the elkhound said. "Do you want to call out your directions from the bank?"

"No," said Rikk, "I'll stay right on your back." He spoke bravely, but in his heart he was almost as frightened of the water as little Petter was.

"Hold tight," said the elkhound. He put his two front feet in the water, and Rikk gulped. The force of the current almost knocked the dog sideways, and Rikk clung tightly to his fur.

In a moment the spray had soaked Rikk completely, but he paid no attention. His whole effort was on keeping the little boy talking.

"Have you ever wanted to meet a troll?" he asked, to make conversation.

"Oh, yes," said Petter. "Mother has promised me that next Christmas I can help with the cream pudding that we always set out for them."

Rikk admired the skill of the elkhound. Even with the strong current pushing him, he managed to keep his body level and his head above water. At last they had reached the log.

"Now listen to me," said Rikk. "I want you to slip down very slowly next to me while I count to ten."

The elkhound remained as motionless as though he were still on dry land, although Rikk knew how hard his feet must be treading water.

Petter looked doubtful for a moment and then he smiled. By the time Rikk had counted to six, the little boy had scrambled to safety on the back of the elkhound. Rikk was so excited that he almost fell into the water himself, and caught hold of the dog's wet fur just in time.

"Good boy," said Rikk, as soon as he had caught his breath. "Now we are all going for a ride."

The trip back seemed much shorter and less frightening, and almost at once they were back at the edge of the water.

"Hold on," said the elkhound to Rikk, "and I will carry you back to the main road. I know what a hurry you are in, and Petter will enjoy the ride."

Rikk kept his hand to his right ear all during the ride so that he could understand what the little boy was saying. Clearly Petter was delighted to have met a troll and kept babbling to him.

"I have a pony," he told Rikk, "and a pet cat. I'll let you help feed my bird if you will come home with me."

"I will be there at Christmastime," Rikk promised. "Will you remember to put out the bowl of cream pudding?"

"It will be a big one," said Petter.

By this time they had reached the road, and the elkhound lay down so that Rikk could get off his back.

"Stay a moment," said the elkhound, looking at him with love in his eyes, "so that we can both thank you."

"No," said Rikk, "I must hurry. I am very late already."

All at once there was a sudden noise, loud and clear. It continued for several seconds, and Rikk's heart sank when he recognized it.

It was the sound of the great bell on the Ringsgaard estate, calling the men in from their work in the fields. And it was the signal to Rikk that by this time he should have reached the crossroads and be on his way home.

He had failed.

Rikk turned in the direction of home and started to trudge his weary way back to the cave, the tears trickling down his cheeks.

His beautiful clothes that he had worn so proudly were wet and muddy. He had failed in the test Spinster Great-aunt Aasve had set for him. And worst of all, he had broken the law of the trolls and been seen by a human being.

His mother had been right. He had not known enough about the world to take his place with the grownups, and when they went out at Christmas for the celebrations he would have to stay behind.

Rikk would not go with them through the snow when they went to visit all the animals at Christmastime, with greetings for the cows and horses and sheep and goats and even for the birds in the trees. He would not look through the windows of the great house and see the human beings gathered around the candlelit pine tree, with presents for each of them and the sled for Petter. He would not see them laughing and excited at Christmas dinner, and he would not take part in the special feast of the trolls when they ate the delicious cream pudding that the mistress of Ringsgaard would set out for them.

And, in summer, there was the celebration on the top of Trond Mountain on Midsummer Eve. There would be a bonfire then, and all sorts of games played by humans and trolls alike. Since the trolls did not let themselves be seen, they could never be caught at their mischief. Sometimes of late years, because of her great age, Spinster Great-aunt Aasve had not attended the Christmas celebrations, but never did she absent herself from the Midsummer Eve festivities on Trond Mountain.

All his life Rikk had looked forward to the day when he would take part in these wonderful things. Today was the day he was to have made himself worthy of them.

As it was, he had to go home and confess he had failed in what he had set out to do. He was wet to the skin. He was hungry and his feet hurt. What he wanted to do was to sit down by the side of the road and weep.

Rikk swallowed hard and plodded on. With a grimy hand he brushed away the few tears that had made their way down his cheek.

After all, he really was twelve years old, and nothing could change that. He was grown up in a way, and grown-up people didn't cry when they were cold and tired. Or whine because they wanted something to eat. Often his parents and the other grownups had been out all night in cold and rainy weather, and when they came back they never complained.

Also, he told himself, the day had not been a complete failure. Many important things had happened to him, and when he was home again he would be able to tell the younger children all about them. He would gather his nieces and nephews and first and second and third cousins around him, and he would hold them spellbound while he told them about his encounter with the wily fox. He would show them how a frog jumped, and how a sparrow flapped his wings and flew. Most miraculous of all, he would tell them that he had actually sat beside a human being, so close that by simply stretching out his hand he was able to touch Petter.

He would teach the smaller children to flap their arms, imitating the wings of the sparrow. They would love to try jump-

ing like a frog. And he would carry the very small ones on his back, pretending that they were Petter and he was the elkhound.

Then he would tell them also about the cricket, and how important it was to be on good terms with him. For of all living creatures, he was the one that brought good luck to anyone he favored.

Not that the cricket had brought very good luck to him. It was all very well to have daydreams, but they were not going to help very much while he stood to listen to what Spinster Great-aunt Aasve was going to say to him.

Rikk was almost home now. He could hear the sound of the waterfall, and he was filled with dread at the thought of having to disappoint all those who had sent him off so hopefully that morning.

Then he reached the entrance of the cave and he could see that the stone door was open so that the entire clan could come out to greet him. Children broke away from their elders and ran to meet him, and Rikk could see the smiles on the faces of his father and mother. He was being received like a conquering hero because he had come home on time, and

almost at once he would have to confess how woefully he had failed them.

Before anyone had a chance to ask questions, Spinster Great-aunt Aasve commanded them all to enter the cave, and Rikk could see that careful preparations had been made for his reception. The elders seated themselves on pillows of cobweb and the children squatted down beside them. Finally Spinster Great-aunt Aasve sat down on the huge stone seat that had been given her by the clan the day she became its mentor and seer. Only Rikk remained standing.

He shifted from one foot to the other. He caught his mother's eye and she smiled at him reassuringly. Then Rikk turned his head and met Spinster Great-aunt Aasve's penetrating gaze.

Rikk drew a long breath. No excuses and no omissions would be tolerated.

He told them everything, how hard he had tried and all the mistakes he had made. And all the time he spoke there was silence in the great hall of the cave.

Then Rikk paused and gathered up all his courage, for he had come to the worst moment of all. He had to tell them the story of the elkhound and how he had talked to little Petter, betraying the law of the trolls. He did not know what the punishment would be.

When he had finished, there was silence in the room.

Rikk shifted from one foot to the other, and finally Spinster Great-aunt Aasve spoke.

"In the first place," she said, "you have spoken the truth, and that is well. You might have pretended to have reached the crossroads, and no one would have known that you failed. In the second place, although you made many mistakes you learned from them all. And in the third place . . ."

She paused for a moment, and Rikk held his breath.

"In the third place, you obeyed the one rule by which all trolls must be guided. You helped a human being in need. It is true that you broke a law of the trolls, but in doing it you obeyed a greater one."

Rikk could hardly believe his eyes. Spinster Great-aunt Aasve was smiling at him.

"In saving the life of little Petter you have proved that you are a true troll of the Rendal clan. We, the grownups, welcome you as one of us."

She came down from her high seat and gave him her hand.

"Oh, thank you," Rikk managed to say as a great wave of happiness spread over him.

"From now on," she said, looking straight in his eyes, "you will enjoy all the privileges of the clan. And you will no longer be known simply as Rikk but will always be addressed as Troll Rikk."

At that moment there was a surging forward of all the trolls. They pressed forward to the spot where he and Spinster Great-aunt Aasve were standing, and the first to reach him were his parents.

"Your mother and I are very proud of you," his father said.

Then came the rest, all speaking at once to tell him how proud they were of him this day. But as Rikk stood there, receiving all this praise, he knew that he himself was the proudest troll in all the Rendal clan.